EARLY BIRD STORIES™

Camping, Here I Come!

Keeping a Budget

Lisa Bullard Illustrated by Mike Byrne

LERNER PUBLICATIONS ◆ MINNEAPOLIS

NOTE TO EDUCATORS

Find text recall questions at the end of each chapter. Critical-thinking and text feature questions are available on page 23. These help young readers learn to think critically about the topic by using the text, text features, and illustrations.

Copyright © 2022 by Lerner Publishing Group, Inc.

All rights reserved. International copyright secured. No part of this book may be reproduced, stored in a retrieval system, or transmitted in any form or by any means—electronic, mechanical, photocopying, recording, or otherwise—without the prior written permission of Lerner Publishing Group, Inc., except for the inclusion of brief quotations in an acknowledged review.

Lerner Publications Company
An imprint of Lerner Publishing Group, Inc.
241 First Avenue North
Minneapolis, MN 55401 USA

For reading levels and more information, look up this title at www.lernerbooks.com.

Photos on p. 22 used with permission of: kriangkrainetnangrong/Shutterstock.com (kid writing); Rawpixel.com/Shutterstock.com (family cleaning); George Rudy/Shutterstock.com (family shopping).

Main body text set in Billy Infant.
Typeface provided by SparkyType.

Library of Congress Cataloging-in-Publication Data

Names: Bullard, Lisa, author. | Byrne, Mike, 1979- illustrator.
Title: Camping, here I come! : keeping a budget / Lisa Bullard ; illustrated by Mike Byrne.
Description: Minneapolis, MN : Lerner Publications Company, [2022] | Series: Money smarts | Includes bibliographical references and index. | Audience: Ages 4-9 | Audience: Grades K-1 | Summary: "Can Kyle sell ten boxes of candy in time to go on his club's camping trip? In this delightful story, readers will learn how to count their money and give the right amount of change"— Provided by publisher.
Identifiers: LCCN 2021001573 (print) | LCCN 2021001574 (ebook) | ISBN 9781728424460 (library binding) | ISBN 9781728438542 (paperback) | ISBN 9781728437972 (ebook)
Subjects: LCSH: Finance—Juvenile literature. | Budget—Juvenile literature. | Selling—Juvenile literature. | Money—Juvenile literature.
Classification: LCC HG173.8 .B85 2022 (print) | LCC HG173.8 (ebook) | DDC 332.4—dc23

LC record available at https://lccn.loc.gov/2021001573
LC ebook record available at https://lccn.loc.gov/2021001574

Manufactured in the United States of America
1-49316-49432-3/2/2021

TABLE OF CONTENTS

Chapter 1
Let's Go Camping.....4

Chapter 2
Selling Candy.....10

Chapter 3
Big Spender.....16

Chapter 4
Camping, Here I Come!.....20

Learn about Money Basics....22

Think about Money Basics:
Critical-Thinking and Text Feature Questions....23

Glossary....24

Learn More....24

Index....24

CHAPTER 1
LET'S GO CAMPING

Our club's going camping.

"Camping costs money," Mr. Jackson said. "We'll track our money with a **budget**."

Budget

Expenses
Campground
Food
Water
Ice
Bug spray
Trash bags
Flashlights
+ Gas for bus
―――――――――
$30 for each camper

"**Expenses** are things we spend money on," he continued. "We have to pay for supplies. It's $30.00 per camper."

"I don't have $30.00," I said.

"That's okay, Kyle. Budgets track income. **Income** is money we take in."

Our club saves money in the bank. Mr. Jackson bought boxes of candy with some of that money.

Each camper gets ten boxes. We'll sell them for income. I'll make $3.00 for each box I sell.

✓ Check! What are Kyle's camping expenses?

CHAPTER 2
SELLING CANDY

At home, my brother put $3.03 on the table.

"Candy, please!" he said.

I gave him back three cents and a box of candy.

The next day, Dad took me out to sell candy.

Mrs. Harding wanted two boxes. "They're $3.00 each," I said. **"Two boxes is $6.00!"**

Ms. Jennings bought one box. She gave me $5.00. I gave her back $2.00. Mr. Spire gave me $3.00 for one box.

✓ Check! How many boxes has Kyle sold?

CHAPTER 3
BIG SPENDER

We tried selling more, but Ms. Clements doesn't eat candy. And Mr. Randall already had some.

Dad said, "I've got an idea.
Let's visit cousin Asheena."

I smiled. "Thanks, Asheena!" She gave me $20.00.

"Eight dollars back," I said.

✓ Check! How much did four boxes of candy cost?

CHAPTER 4
CAMPING, HERE I COME!

Dad bought my last box of candy. I gave him back the $10.00 I owed him.

I made $30.00!
Camping, here I come!

✓ Check! Who bought Kyle's last candy box?

LEARN ABOUT MONEY BASICS

Many people save their money in a bank. Money is safe in a bank.

Write out your expenses and income in a notebook. This will help you keep track of your money.

Do you have any income? It could be money you get for chores or an allowance. Or it could be money you get as a gift.

Before you go shopping, think about your budget. This will help you know how much money you have to spend.

There are four types of coins people commonly use in the US. Quarters are 25 cents, dimes are 10 cents, nickels are 5 cents, and pennies are 1 cent.

THINK ABOUT MONEY BASICS: CRITICAL-THINKING AND TEXT FEATURE QUESTIONS

How does your family budget money?

Who is this book's illustrator?

Where do you save your money?

What page does chapter 1 start on?

Expand learning beyond the printed book. Download free, complementary educational resources for this book from our website, www.lerneresource.com.

GLOSSARY

bills: paper money

budget: a way to keep track of the money being taken in and the money being spent

expense: something that money is spent on

income: money that is taken in, such as gifts or money earned

LEARN MORE

Budgeting Money
https://www.ducksters.com/money/budgeting_money.php

Bullard, Lisa. *It All Adds Up: Earning Money.* Minneapolis: Lerner Publications, 2022.

Waxman, Laura Hamilton. *Let's Explore Earning Money.* Minneapolis: Lerner Publications, 2019.

INDEX

bank, 8

budget, 5, 7

expenses, 6

income, 7, 9

selling, 9, 12, 14–17